A CHILD OF A VETERAN
Thank You for Your Service

by Larisa E. Owen, PhD

gatekeeper press
Columbus, Ohio

This book is a work of fiction. The names, characters and events in this book are the products of the author's imagination or are used fictitiously. Any similarity to real persons living or dead is coincidental and not intended by the author.

The views and opinions expressed in this book are solely those of the author and do not necessarily reflect the views or opinions of Gatekeeper Press. Gatekeeper Press is not to be held responsible for and expressly disclaims responsibility of the content herein.

A Child of a Veteran: Thank You for Your Service

Published by Gatekeeper Press
2167 Stringtown Rd., Suite 109
Columbus, OH 43123-2989
www.GatekeeperPress.com

Copyright © 2022 by Larisa E. Owen PhD

All rights reserved. Neither this book, nor any parts within it may be sold or reproduced in any form or by any electronic or mechanical means, including information storage and retrieval systems, without permission in writing from the author. The only exception is by a reviewer, who may quote short excerpts in a review.

Library of Congress Control Number: 2022938517

ISBN (hardcover): 9781662927423
ISBN (paperback): 9781662927430
eISBN: 9781662927447

"Goal! Well done, Nick!" Coach beamed at Nick before blowing the whistle to end practice. Nick stayed to pick up the soccer balls and help Coach tidy up. Nick was happy to see Ashley, his friend from next door, slowly beginning to walk home.

"Wait up, Ash!" he called, jogging after her.

Ashley smiled when she saw him. "Thought I'd missed you; everyone else went ages ago!"

"I was helping Coach."

"You're so good at things like that—" Ashley was interrupted by a shout from across the road.

"How's your mom, Ashley? Is she coming home soon?"

"She's fine. Thanks, Coach Gardner. She will finally come home this week!"

"Excellent! Thank her for her service, from me. And thanks to you too, by the way. Thank you for *your* service."

Ashley waved, and they continued walking. Ashley's mom is in the military. Nick fell quiet after a while. His dad, James, had been in the military too! Nick remembered that he had hardly seen his dad from the age of two until he was five. But, no one ever thanked Nick for *his* sacrifice because his dad had served in the military, and now he is a veteran.

That weekend, Ashley and her mom Mitzi came to take Nick to the movies.

Ashley said, "Mom, look. The sign says 'Military Families Welcome'!"

Mitzi showed her military card, and the attendant said, "Thank you for your service." Then he looked at Ashley and said, "Thank you, young girl, for *your* service too." Nick smiled, paid for his snacks, and they all went into the theater.

The next day, Nick's dad had to go to see the doctor. He had hurt his knee while he was in the United States Marine Corps and needed treatment. Nick went along too, watching his dad stretching out his painful knee. The doctor was very happy with James's hard work. "Well done!" she said. "And by the way, thank you for your service!" She glanced at Nick as though about to say something but didn't.

On Veterans Day, James and Nick went to a shelter to help feed homeless veterans. Seeing the line of people, Nick felt very sad. "Why don't they have homes, Dad?" he asked.

"Being in the military can be very hard. It's a big change being home again, and sometimes veterans' families need help. Those of us who have something to give should give it or be a helper like we're doing now." Nick shook his head sadly. "But, why don't they get the help they need, Dad?" Dad said, "Sometimes, when veterans return home, they don't get that help. It can be really hard on them and their families."

In history class on Monday, the teacher mentioned Iraq. She looked expectantly at Ashley.

"Ashley? Did your mom go to Iraq?"

Ashley nodded her head yes. Nick raised his hand.

"My dad served in Iraq," he said. "He was in Desert Storm."

Nick's teacher smiled. "Oh, Nick, that's wonderful. Please, thank your dad for his service." And then she walked over to Nick and said, "And thank you, too, for your service, Nick. I'm glad you told us about your dad."

It got her thinking. The next day, Nick's history teacher went to see the school principal and asked, "Why do we only ask if parents are in the military now and not ask about family members who served in the past?"

The principal sighed and shrugged. "The form we have to fill in only asks for parents that are in the military today, not veterans. I never thought of that. It's just the way the form asks the question. We'll see what we can do about that."

The next day, Nick and his friend Vielka were invited to have dinner over at Ashley's house.

Ashley asked her mother, "Mommy, how come people thank you, me, and Nick's dad for our service, but they never thank Nick?"

Ashley's mom explained, "People should thank Nick because when you take your uniform off and you become a veteran, that veteran's family should be appreciated too. So, Nick, *thank you for your service!*"

Nick smiled and felt proud.

Vielka said to Nick, "Hey, my mom is a veteran too."

Nick turned to Vielka and said, "Well, thank you for *your* service."

Later that evening, Nick was getting ready for bed when Dad came into his room. "Ready for bed, champ?"

Nick smiled. "Hey, Dad, why do people only ask about military kids and forget about veterans' kids? You served your country just like Ashley's mom, but it's like I don't matter now that you're a veteran!"

James looked at Nick and said, "I am not sure, Nick. Ashley's mom serves in the military just like I did. So, both you and Ashley are military kids. You and Ashley should also be thanked for your service in the same way. So, I think you should be thanked for your service too."

James gave him a hug. "You're right, son," he said. "The children of veterans should be recognized, proud, and even thanked for their strength, just like military kids. Children of veterans may need help dealing with having parents who could have problems as a result of serving their country."

Nick smiled. "Thank you, Dad. I'm going to keep asking why, and hopefully, more kids like me—sons and daughters of veterans—will be thanked in the future."

How can we all make sure that the children of veterans are not invisible?

That night, Nick snuggled into bed, not knowing that he had set wheels in motion. The boy lay in his bed and thought, *How can I make sure people appreciate military kids but also remember veterans' kids?*

As Nick slipped off to dreamland, he looked out his window. The stars and moon shone brightly, and Nick whispered to himself, "I bet there are so many ways I can help make people understand about veterans' kids like me!"

Nick came up with many ideas. There was a lot to do.

Thanks to all children of veterans!

Do you have ideas on how Nick and Ashley can help people understand about the children of veterans? Would you like to be a part of the second book about the children of veterans? Go to www.childrenofveterans.us and tell us your ideas. If your idea is chosen, a donation will be made in your name to the charity of your choice.

ABOUT THE AUTHOR

Dr. Owen is the wife of a Marine Corps veteran who served in Desert Storm, the daughter of an Army veteran, and the mother of a child of a veteran.

www.ingramcontent.com/pod-product-compliance
Lightning Source LLC
LaVergne TN
LVHW071655060526
838200LV00030B/474